BENNY THE BUNNY AND HIS BIG FLOPPY EARS

Benny The Bunny Book 1

Rachel McKay

CHAPTER 1

Benny was running as fast his four little legs could carry him. He had to keep going. He couldn't go back now.

He came to a sudden stop as he saw a large bush and dived in under it. They would never see him here. Or would they?

A few seconds later, Benny was running again. His heart was pounding, his little legs were getting sore, and his ears were bouncing up and down. But he couldn't stop now.

They were gaining on him. The humans' voices were getting louder. They were shouting and calling his name as they waved their lights around and carried their plastic carry cases. They were trying to catch him. They were trying to take him back to the animal rescue. But Benny wasn't going back. No way.

'Over here!'

Benny couldn't believe his ears. Was that a rabbit's voice? He had heard about rabbits living in the wild before, but he'd never expected to meet one.

'Over here!' the voice called again. This time Benny was sure of it, that voice definitely belonged to another rabbit. He quickly changed direction and started running towards it.

He dived down the hole and the other rabbit dived in after him. 'Shhh' whispered the other bunny and put her paw over Benny's mouth, 'don't say a thing or they'll hear you!'. For what felt like ages, the two little bunnies waited just inside the burrow for the voices to move away. When at last they did, Benny let out a sigh of relief. He had done it. He was free.

CHAPTER 2

Benny woke up the next morning to five little faces right in front of his. It took the little rabbit a second to remember where he was, but when he did, he was suddenly a very happy little rabbit.

'So, you're awake'. Benny tried

to sit up but the five little bunnies were much too interested in him to move away. 'Come on you five' the voice said and as the baby rabbits turned to hop away, Benny saw the bunny from last night hopping towards him. Benny sat up, smiled and stretched out his right front paw. 'I'm Benny' he said, 'what's your name?'

'I told you last night, you don't

remember?', the other rabbit asked. Seeing the blank look on Benny's face, she realised that he didn't remember their talk the night before. She wasn't surprised though, the number of times he'd bumped his head on the top of the burrow last night. He'd clearly never done this before! 'Well, I'm Milly' she said and put her paw in Benny's.

The baby bunnies were starting to fall asleep that morning as Benny and his new friend hopped through the tunnels, and went outside. Milly would usually never be seen outside during the day, but she needed to talk to Benny alone, and the little ones needed their rest.

Benny and his new friend talked all morning. He'd never talked to another rabbit this much before. Whenever he'd made a friend at the animal rescue, they always seemed to leave, and he was always left behind.

He told Milly about his life at the animal rescue, and how no one ever liked him as much as the other bunnies. He told her how everyone always laughed at his ears and how he was never going to find a home. And then he told her how happy he was that he was going to live with her now.

CHAPTER 3

'You want to stay here?' Milly asked, taken aback. 'With us? Forever?'. Benny nodded, grinning. 'Yes!' he said and gave his new friend a big hug.

Milly didn't know what to say. Benny was a nice bunny, but he couldn't stay here! He wasn't wild like they were, he could never survive in the wild. She also knew that her big sister Molly would never agree.

'Well...' Milly said slowly, 'emm...' she paused, trying to think how to break the news to her new friend. 'We'd better ask Molly about that'.

Benny hadn't met Molly yet, but he couldn't wait. If she was anything like Milly, he was sure they were going to get on great.

'Come in' Molly called when Milly knocked on the twigs at the doorway to Molly's burrow. Molly was the boss rabbit of the warren, so she had the biggest burrow, right in the middle of the warren, and no one was allowed in without asking.

'You what!?' Molly stood up tall on her back legs and looked right at the little grey bunny in front of her. 'You want to stay here? I don't think that's going to work!

Benny's face fell and his bottom lip started to wobble. 'You mean I can't stay?' he asked his voice starting to shake as he tried not to cry.

CHAPTER 4

Benny was on the move again. Molly had said that he wouldn't fit in with the rest of the bunnies in the warren, and Benny had been so upset that he'd just had to leave. It was because of his big ears. He was sure of it. He'd never liked his over-sized ears, but he really hated them now. Just when he'd finally found a home, and found a friend, his big floppy ears had ruined it for him.

Benny froze as he heard a noise behind him. What was that? As he stood up and twitched his little nose, his eyes widened and he gasped. 'A fox!' he squeaked and took off running as fast as he could. He'd been hopping for hours now and his little legs were already worn out, but he didn't have a choice.

The fox was getting closer now, and as Benny took a quick glance over his shoulder, he could see he was never going to outrun it. His little body was so sore, from his paws to his tail, and he just could not run any faster. What he would give now to be back in his room at the animal rescue, or to be back in the burrow with Milly. 'Oh, I wish I'd never left!' he cried as he ran.

'Benny!' The little rabbit picked up his head as he heard a familiar voice. 'Milly?' he called back. Looking around for his friend. He'd been running for hours now, what was she doing so far away from her home? 'Milly!?' he called again.

'Over here' she called, and Benny once again, ran towards his friend's voice. He was running through the woods now, and it was getting harder and harder to dodge all the trees, logs and bushes in his way. 'Milly?!' he called again, still not able to see his friend. 'In here Benny!' she called back, and as Benny turned to his right, he could see his little friend's head sticking between the spars of an old wooden fence.

CHAPTER 5

Benny had just squeezed through the fence when the fox crashed into it. 'Phew!' he sighed and flopped down on the ground. 'You alright Benny?' Milly asked as she sat down beside her friend. The fox pawed at the ground on the other side of the fence, but deciding not to jump it, turned and went on it's way.

Benny nodded 'yeah…. I'm …. alright' he said trying to catch his breath. 'We were all so worried about you!' Milly said, 'Even Molly was upset. Why did you run off like that?' The little grey bunny had been so relieved to get away from the fox that for a minute, he had forgotten all his problems. 'She said I wouldn't fit in with all of you' Benny replied, 'I know it's because of my ears'. His eyes started to fill up with tears again. 'Everyone hates them'.

'Don't be silly Benny' Milly said, smiling and putting her paw on her friend's back. 'It wasn't because of your ears. It's just that well, it would be really hard for you to live in the wild like we do'. Benny stopped crying and turned to look at his friend. 'You mean, you don't hate my ears?' he asked. 'Of course not, Benny, it doesn't matter that you look different from us, we just don't think you would like living in the wild very much'.

Benny was about to protest, but then he remembered what had just happened. 'I suppose you're right Milly' he said, 'It's a lot harder than you'd think!'

CHAPTER 6

Benny was so glad to feel safe again when he lay down in the burrow that night. The rest of the rabbits were out looking for food, but because he was so tired, he'd come inside to have a lie down first. A part of Benny wished he could stay here, in the burrow, all of his life. But he knew that Milly and Molly were right. He just wasn't cut out for life in the wild. Still, they had said he could stay here for a few days until he had time to come up with a plan.

Benny woke later that night, stretched, and headed out of the burrow. When he got above ground, he hopped over to Milly who was munching on some grass nearby. 'Hi Benny' she said as he hopped up to her, 'want some?' Benny tucked into the grass next to his friend.

'Benny!' The little grey bunny turned to look at his friend. Milly had stopped eating and was standing straight up, with her ears sticking straight up in the air. 'I've had an idea!'

'What?' Benny asked, wondering what the wild rabbit was

so excited about. 'See that garden we hid in yesterday?' She paused, but not for long enough to give Benny the chance to answer. 'Well, the humans there are really nice and let us eat from their garden all the time.' Benny gave Milly a funny look, not sure where she was going with this. 'Well they must like rabbits, so I bet they would let you live with them!" Milly started jumping up and down in the air, very pleased with her idea.

Benny just stared at her. Could she be right? Would these humans be nice to him? Would they really let him live with them?

The little bunny had wanted a home for so long. Was he finally going to have one?

CHAPTER 7

They had been waiting for the humans for ages now, but no one seemed to be coming. Milly and Benny were just about to give up and go back to the warren when they heard footsteps and the house door opened.

Up until now Benny had been

feeling quite good about the idea, but now that the humans were actually coming, he was starting to feel a bit less brave. 'Are you sure about this?' he leaned over and whispered in Milly's ear. 'Of course' she whispered back, 'it's a great idea!'

They had stayed up all day yesterday planning this, and Benny knew what he had to do. As soon as the first human stepped out the door, he was going to hop right over to them, stand up as tall as he could on his back legs, and do his very best to ask them if he could come and live with them.

They just didn't seem to be getting it. Not just one, but two, humans had now come out the door, and neither of them seemed to understand what he was trying to ask them. They were just standing there, staring at him!

'Katy!' called one of the tall humans as she opened the house door and went back inside. 'At last!' Benny thought. He was really getting fed up waiting for them to answer his question, but at least they seemed to be getting somewhere.

A couple of minutes later a small human came out of the

door and bent down in front of Benny. 'Hello little man!' she said. Benny had never been called that before, but the girl's voice sounded friendly, so he decided he could get used to that name. 'Hello!' he said back happily. He wasn't sure if the girl could understand him or not, but he wanted to be nice, just in case.

The girl talked to him for a

couple of minutes, and then she said just what Benny had been waiting to hear. 'You want to stay here tonight little man?' Benny was so excited that he started jumping up and down. For some reason this seemed to make the humans laugh, but Benny was too happy to care. He had a home!

CHAPTER 8

That night was the best one of Benny's entire life. The humans had spent the afternoon making a huge space for him to play in, and getting their shed ready for him to live in. He had loads of hay, loads of toys, and best of all, he had a real home.

After saying goodbye to Milly he'd spent the whole night zooming around and playing with all his new stuff. Now that the sun was rising, he was exhausted.

The little grey bunny was just drifting off to sleep that morning when he heard voices coming towards him. At first he thought it was just his new humans, but then he heard another voice as well. Benny jumped up. 'I know that voice!'. It was one of the humans from the animal rescue.

How did they know he was here? Were they going to take him away? Benny was so scared, and so upset at the same time. After all this time he'd finally found a home, and now he was going to lose it. As the humans started to open the shed door Benny stamped his back feet off the shed floor as hard as he could. He had to call for help. Maybe Milly was around, maybe she would be able to help him again.

Benny had been thumping for a few minutes now, but Milly didn't seem to be coming. He could tell the humans were talking about him, but they were too fast for him to make out what they were say-ing. They were making plans to catch him though. He was sure of it. All of a sudden though, they all turned and walked away. Benny stopped thumping. What were they all doing?

CHAPTER 9

Benny took his chance and dived under the big pile of hay in the corner of the shed. If they couldn't find him, they couldn't catch him. And if they couldn't catch him, they couldn't take him back.

'You alright little man?'

Benny peeked out through the hay to see the girl human looking right at him. How did she know he was in here? He slowly stepped out, shook they hay off of himself, and moved towards the girl. She seemed nice and she seemed to understand him better than the tall humans did, so maybe he'd be able to tell her how he felt about going back to the animal rescue.

Seeing the worried look on the little rabbit's face, Katy stretched out her hand and gently stroked his furry head. 'It's ok little one, you don't have to go with them' Benny's eyes widened again, this time in surprise. 'Yes' she laughed seeing the look on his face 'that's right, you can stay here with me'. Benny couldn't believe his ears. He really had found his home.

Benny drifted off to sleep later that morning, a very happy little rabbit.

To join Benny and his friends
on more adventures, visit:

www.furryfriendsbooks.com

Here you'll be able to:
- Join the Furry Friends
Book Club
- Download free activities
- Find out about new
Furry Friends books
- and much more!

BOOKS BY THIS AUTHOR

Henry The Hamster Escapes

Henry the hamster is fed up living in tiny his little cage, so with the help of his new friend Mimi the mouse, he comes up with a plan!

Printed in Great Britain
by Amazon